# Perks, Politics and Pandemonium

Tales of Modern Society-
18 'storeys' high

UMA SARANGAN

INDIA · SINGAPORE · MALAYSIA

ISBN 979-8-89133-797-8

अयं बन्धुरयं नेति गणना लघुचेतसाम् ।
उदारचरितानां तु वसुधैव कुटुम्बकम् ॥

English Translation

"This one is a relative, friend and brother;

this other one is an outlander" is for the mean-minded.

For those who're known as magnanimous,

the entire world constitutes but a family.

## *Monkey, Man or Human – Whose lineage is it anyway?*

*O' it is a circus of sorts, man's antics in a modern society*
*That a monkey would grasp not, with its prehensile tail,*
*But it can go farther, than those high storeys, you see!*
*The simian cousins bind and bond, the instincts to survive*
*As a herd, to thrive in the wild, in the prey 'n' predator games –*
*To look out for the other, sans the power 'n' hunger games*

*The monkey brains laid threadbare, baring the complex human genome -*
*The successor of modern society - MAN at the apex of the evolutionary dome*
*The mould of culture 'n' civilization – it's a miasma of a never-ending craze -*
*Who is the big 'n' tall, the mightiest of all - is ever the conquest spearheaded*
*Superseding all human rights - the basics of being human, beheaded*
*The human gene - the lineage of humanity, the expression of humanness –*
*Entrapped in a mind - a mushroom of mindlessness -*

*An intellect that unravels mysteries of the universe, lies benumbed*
*When it comes to speak out- the power of speech succumbs*
*To the voice of the crowd, that empathy in the cloud of the mob*
*Even when a fellow turns predator or is preyed upon,*
*the rest simply collapses into a blob!*

*So, even as buildings soar higher than the tallest trees of the wild*
*As the brainchild of man, in fineries no mild*
*Will the finesse set apart the man from the monkey,*
*or the human from the monster?*
*There is no telling of the hidden Frankenstein,*
*that only a man can breed and enshrine!*
*A monkey might still climb over those high storeys of the man-made*
*But for a man to climb down from those heights*
*To meet his human self - would he contrive a "gravity(bound)-flight"?*

# Contents

# Glossary

- Aamney-saamney/Padosi – Next-door neighbour
- Ghar ghar ban gaya Shauchalaya – Every home has turned into a public toilet
- Bahus – daughters-in-law
- Aam aadmi – Common man
- Maryaada Purushottam – Virtues-personified, the best of men (reference to Lord Ram from Hindu mythology)
- Ekpatnivrata – pledged to be married to one wife alone
- Vijaypath – Route to victory
- Cheeni – Sugar
- Amrutha Kalasha – Pitcher containing nectar of immortality
- Mahayudh – Epic war
- Sanskaari – cultured, tradition-bound
- Shakti – feminine(divine) prowess of the universe

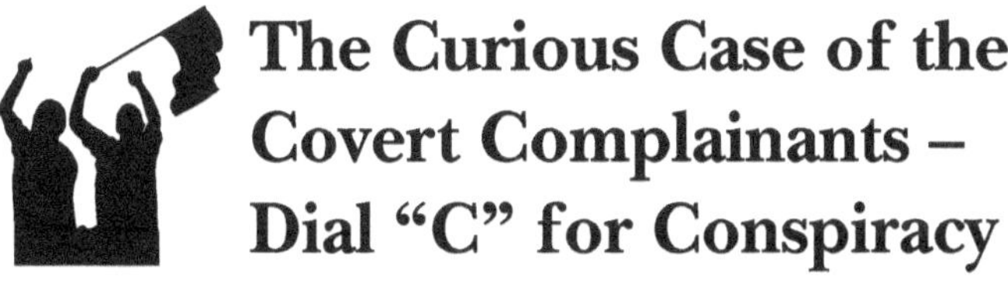

# The Curious Case of the Covert Complainants – Dial "C" for Conspiracy

"I am a WOMAN, I too have a daughter!", she thundered with murderous rage at Srivatsan. Rudy, her comrade, was stomping around, claiming to protect women's rights. He donned the champion of women's cause, elucidating that he was one of the chieftains of the sexual harassment committee in his "IT bigwig" company. Srivatsan had addressed Rudy thus, "I have a high school daughter. Do you think I don't respect women?"

Urmila was within the perimeter of the pandemonium that was happening in her apartment's clubhouse. She was within earshot as the voices roared one on top of the other. She was wondering whether to barge in and prevent the impending physical combat. Her husband, Srivatsan, who had delivered in the role of Association Treasurer, was being accused of misconduct with the facility management lady staff. This was extremely shocking, as Srivatsan had nominated himself for running the tenure in the next committee. The nomination was done a month prior. And the GBM for announcing the new MC was only a fortnight away.

Urmila's thoughts raced like a bullet train retracing the two-year-long sojourn of Srivatsan as an MC member—how Srivatsan had unfailingly delivered to his role, going beyond his scope to attend to the works, activities, and crises centred around high-storey apartment complexes in the city of Bengaluru. On the face of it, the team seemed to function like Ocean's 8, but for the occasional ego clashes, the not-so-occasional bickering, and the theatrics of incidents (from intoxicated residents swooning in common areas to footloose rats in the basement), all of which had become a mainstay of apartment living. Srivatsan used to share the updates with her on a daily basis. To Urmila's imaginative mind, these incidents always provided a muse to write about. Then, "What could have gone abominably wrong to disrupt the team dynamics?", Urmila muttered to herself.

But before her train of thought could move further along the two-year-long journey of Srivatsan, she found its carriages derailing and tumbling down an abyss. She was jolted back to the present when she heard a booming voice. The drama unfolded in typical Bollywood style, where the mafia loomed large over the captive whistleblower or the *aam aadmi*, and circled around him, rubbing their palms and flipping fully loaded pistols on their fingertips. The "She" speaker of the MC was thumping her chest and ranting, "We are trying to protect your family. YOU HAVE to resign!" To which Srivatsan calmly responded, "I have not done anything wrong. It is a false allegation. You must investigate those two ladies once again." He continued, "I repeat, it was because of shouting at them for loitering on the premises. They are trying to seek revenge. I have been with you for two years, working with lady staff from other facility management services. No complaint had surfaced then. How do you give credence to these allegations from employees who are just two months old in our system?"

He turned to Rudy and spoke, "I have a high school-going daughter. Do you think I would treat any woman in such a way? It's unbelievable that you are not giving it a third-eye appraisal. I am being implicated", Srivatsan remonstrated calmly. Then the "She" and Rudy flipped out their gadgets as if they were unravelling a secret ninja wheel weapon that caught its victim unaware. Excerpts of voice recordings were played. They declared, "WE have evidence! YOU CANNOT DENY THIS, CAN YOU?" Srivatsan was dismayed. The recordings were those of the preliminary discussions, which were casual conversations with the "She" and the president of the committee. Urmila later learned that Srivatsan was NOT one bit aware that those conversations were recorded.

The mastermind behind the entire operation, the President of the MC, whom Urmila derisively referred to as "Snape" (for his sly, slithering behaviour), remained mute. The other eight members continued to pound Srivatsan with their unintelligible utterances; the chorus rant that emerged out of it was "Step down from the elections, Srivatsan, or else we will expose your misconduct. Think of your family. We want to protect your family." Then the "She" passed the most scathing remark: "I showed your wife to my husband the other day, when at the park. You know what he said? That he pities her." At this point, Urmila clenched her fists and wanted to barge in and punch the "She" right in the face. But she had assured Srivatsan that she would exercise restraint and that her presence would not be visible.

What appalled Urmila was not the political gambit of the proceedings, but the animosity and vendetta that were rubbing its ugly face against a fellow resident—in this instance, Srivatsan. It was the "DO or DIE" mantra being drilled into Srivatsan's head. "STEP DOWN!" rang in loud in the air that filled that large space in the club house, where the 'Ocean's 8' had gathered. As for

Srivatsan, he did not want to yield. For one, it would imply that he is in assent to the allegations, and secondly, both Urmila and he strongly felt that "one should not go silently into the night without a fight!" The allegations were being threaded together to levy charges of "sexual harassment." The WhatsApp exchange between the accuser namely the supervising lady staff from Facility Management Services(FMS) and Srivatsan was being exacerbated without giving it a factual background. The sting operations carried out against Srivatsan, which generated voice recordings, were based on freewheeling conversations with the "She" and Snape without the entirety of the context. The recorded conversations, as relayed to Urmila later, were "entrapping" and doctored to seek the answers that the "Dynamic duo" (Snape and the "She" pair) wanted to hear. The statements would later be used as "self-confessing" evidence.

# The Plot Thickens…

Urmila could imagine the degree of conspiracy that would have been involved in the hatching—the mission to just preempt Srivatsan from standing for the elections. In all the preceding meetings centred around this issue, political drama aside, there were many pertinent queries that left Urmila flummoxed. She left her hideout post in the clubhouse in a hurry and waited for Srivatsan to return home. When he did and they settled down, Urmila raised her concerns: "Vats, how can they give more credibility to those two ladies' statements? You have been with this team for more than two years. The previous facility management company also had female staff. There were no such issues that cropped up."

Vats nodded in assent and added, "You see, Urmi, they must have been planning this for a long time to kick me out. Firstly, I am the only one who does not blindly accept whatever they say. So, to say I was never a part of their group, neither did I pledge allegiance to their larger social cluster."

Urmila was still not convinced and went on, "But Vats, why stoop to such a low level? Fabricate such a lowly accusation. I mean, based on *WhatsApp exchanges,* this is not acceptable. Why aren't those ladies being investigated independently?"

Srivatsan, flailing his arms, snapped, "See, they have the backing of their clout—members from the previous

MC. After all, you do know that all the members, leaving aside me and your friend's husband, were hand-picked by that group to form the association for the year 2020. I was the only outlier!"

Urmila continued, "But you went the extra mile to deliver your duty. What more would they have needed? But most of all, how could they record conversations without your consent? Unless it is a matter of national security, voice or video recordings are strictly illegal, am I correct? That too, in that excerpt of the first recording of your discussion, the "SHE" conveniently framed the questions in such a manner that the background and context are not brought into the picture."

Srivatsan seemed plunged into deep thought as Urmila looked questioningly and prodded. He spoke a few minutes later: "Come to think of it, if we were to piece it together, it was perfectly orchestrated. The incoming of this new FMS which Snape pitched for. Leveraging the two lady staff to lodge complaints against me. Obviously, the FMS company is a puppet in the hands of Snape!"

"Those two ladies are, moreover, now vaulted securely under Snape's protection. Even if you, me, or any other owner of the apartment want to get the facts straight, they won't speak up. But first of all, we won't be allowed to be anywhere within their perimeter. Snape and his team (and whoever is behind this) are just hellbent on ensuring that I am not part of the next MC."

Urmila interjected here as she tried to marshal her thoughts on what Srivatsan had regaled her on the chain of events up until this meeting. "Vats, why did that housekeeping lady frame you when she was in need of financial help and expressed so? She had asked you whether the money from selling the scrap could be used. All that you did was offer her that sum so that she did not end up getting into a financial imbroglio, like siphoning off that cash from the association. Haven't you mentioned that the earnings from scrap disposal are also part of the association's accounted money?"

"Urmi," Srivatsan spoke resignedly, "these housekeeping staff, as I had mentioned earlier, were not diligent in delivering their duties. They were loitering on the premises instead of supervising or monitoring the activities. So, I screamed at them in one instance. My point is, that if we don't train them now, they will never do it properly, and maintenance will go for a toss. In all probability, these two ladies wanted to avenge my screaming at them. The timing of that incident was perfect for Snape to put his diabolical plan into action."

"Ahem, Vats, you should never have trusted these people," Urmila regretfully noted, "the "She" and Snape, especially during that first discussion. You very well know how Snape has always managed to convince others in that team with his contrivances, be it any issue. If you recall, the ouster of "Lady Blue" from your team. Wasn't Snape the master brain behind it? Of course, there was no maligning or drama. But still, between the two of us, we agreed that Lady Blue was wronged."

"You are right," Srivatsan muttered under his breath. "I should not have lent a sympathetic ear to those ladies from the Facility Management too. Instead of being conducive to their issues, I should have taken the primary stand against their unprofessional behaviour and reported them. But I did not want to jeopardise their career. As I told you before, such a taint on their reputation would mean a blot on their career path as well."

"Well, now, thanks to them, your integrity is under question, your character has been assassinated, and your public image has been tarnished. How will we continue living here?" Urmila spoke in a tone of exasperation.

"Don't talk like that, Urmi. If we bow out, it will imply that we are in the wrong. Anyways, we have taken the legal course of action", Srivatsan said assuredly. He continued," We are now abiding by what the lawyer says. But yes, he has advised us not to let any of these crooks know about our legal recourse."

"Let's see, Vats." replied Urmila distractedly, as she fumbled through the resident WhatsApp groups pensively. Her thoughts were on a roller coaster ride of sorts—a zillion "what if" scenarios were plummeting down from the highest arch of the coaster ride, right into the pit of her stomach, regurgitating a million-dollar question: "Were there secret ties between Snape and the Facility Management company? Were these ladies established as pawns right from the beginning just to entrap Vats? Did Snape himself have a special bond with that complainant lady?"

The roller coaster in Urmila's mind did not stop. It went zipping on the tracks of "When It All Began", trundling at stretches, then oscillating steadily about its mean position, to the infamous Snape, whose long residence in the society had etched a mark in the history of PMS society. At this juncture, Urmila found herself disembarking a monument of the seven-year-old political history of PMS that embodied not only Snape but also the long list of dissident residents at that time. To this date, this invisible monument has been a glaring testimony to the fiercest battles that have been unleashed in the history of residential communities, from the WhatsApp orators to the silent operators who would work incognito and the martyrs who were hushed into oblivion. Seven years ago, when Urmila had just moved into society, the political atmosphere at that time seemed like a crucible for "Operation Bluestar" with the mission to wipe out the "militia" and establish a democracy in society.

Who were the 'militia' and what was the dissidents' uprising about?

# Seven years ago... The Uprising of 2017 to Overthrow 'Raavan Raj'

"Hey Urmila, nice to see you down. Settled in?" Urmila stopped right there on her walking track to see one of the 'political activists' of the apartment addressing her.

It had been just a week since she moved in with her kids. Srivatsan's contract in the Middle East was for another year, which meant that she would have to run the show solo even in their new home. So, as in her previous apartment, where she had a thriving social network, she was eager to meet new people and make friends. But in view of the political turmoil, which she learned about later, the environs were not exactly hospitable to a new resident. So, apart from the chance interactions with neighbours, Urmila was yet to become familiar with the larger PMS family. But of course, WhatsApp came to the rescue as a kindly neighbourhood messenger when people stayed indoors or could not take time out for their *aamney-samney* chitchat. Thus, she had extended her circle of acquaintances (not her immediate neighbours) through WhatsApp exchanges, one of whom was a prime-time activist who was stalling her walking at present. Urmila turned back to reply, "Hey Mala, yes, sort of." It was a quick exchange of pleasantries before they parted ways. Urmila discovered that her acquaintance's activism on WhatsApp groups knew no bounds and therefore gave her the epithet of 'Randy Raccoon' for flippant verbiage and 'steal-the-limelight' gimmicks that came into play in the coming months.

A month had elapsed since this meeting, and Urmila had just gotten to interact with "Randy Raccoon" and her bestie. She was fumbling through her WhatsApp groups, lying in bed. There was not much that she could do, as she was put on complete bed rest by her yoga doctor. Urmila was diagnosed with a crippling spinal condition that did not give her much scope for movement. The phone and its apps had become her stay-at-home companion, with the WhatsApp groups being a single window to the outside world of her apartment.

While she was tossing and turning in her bed with great difficulty, the doorbell rang. When her kids answered the door and announced the visitor, it was quite a surprise for Urmila to have an unexpected visitor. She managed to extricate herself from bed and, with great difficulty, staggered towards the living room.

"Urmila, sorry to come in unannounced. I have not seen you for more than a month now. Hope all is well." It was Randy Raccoon who had made herself comfortable on the living room couch.

Urmila winced and smiled at the same time, as her standing posture was making her spine crunch and creak, like singing a duet. She replied, "Not so well. I have been on bed rest for a month now. Would you mind if we went to my room and chit-chatted? I really cannot withstand standing or sitting for long."

Randy Raccoon nodded vigorously in assent. "Sure, sure, let's go over to your room." Both Urmila and Randy went to the bedroom, where Urmila simply lay on her back and asked Randy to make herself comfortable too.

"So, what is up, Mala? Glad to see you after a long time!" Randy exclaimed, "What on earth happened to you, Urmila?"

"Oh well, it is a case of a prolapsed disc, and I have been advised complete bed rest for the next two months by my yoga doctor. Talk about awry lifestyles and cranky spines! Enough about me. Tell me what is up at your end. What is happening in our apartment?"

Randy regaled about several instances of the so-called "atrocities" perpetrated by the Adcom, the de facto ruling party who had taken charge of sealing all open ends with the building's maintenance company, before the complete takeover. The Adcom was spearheaded by four highly active, responsive, and overreactive members who established their regime in the residents' WhatsApp and other social media groups; they were the "Fantastic Four." However, what seemed to cast an eclipse on their hard work and honourable deeds was their autocratic approach. Urmila had gotten a whiff of it in the residents' WhatsApp groups. Be it having the last word on any discussion or dismissing other residents' opinions who were not part of their clout, the "Fantastic Four" modus operandi was visible.

Urmila found Randy's narrative entertaining in some parts and quite disturbing in some instances. To what extent she could be involved was another question altogether. But for the time being, the talk and the information deluge took her mind off the excruciating pain she was undergoing. No doubt, she could not take every aspect of Randy's side of the story at face value. After all, no strife erupts without the mutual participation of the warring parties. And, yes, when it came to offence or defence, by these parties, the general stance was 'holier than thou'.

Randy went to great lengths with the nitty-gritty details of the autocratic regime of the Adcom: not respecting boundaries, zero decorum, and a lack of open-mindedness, to name a few. Urmila interjected here with a smirk. "Yes, I have noticed their self-propaganda antics. Our nation's political parties can take a lesson or two from these people about building a public social media image."

Randy ranted on, unmindful of what Urmila had to say. It was not just social media representation that the Fantastic Four had in PMS. They seemed to be slowly monopolising governance without a sense of inclusiveness. Any voice of dissent or random behaviour was responded to with a barrage of mail, WhatsApp messages, and public ostracising on the ground and in the common residents' groups.

To cut a long story short, the Adcom was projected as the "ten-headed" Raavan, who, if not overthrown, would turn PMS into a veritable Lanka.

With an epic narrative delivered with fervour, Randy sighed heavily and got ready to leave, but not without a closing statement: "Adcom rule must end if sanity, peace, and humanity have to be preserved in PMS."

"Take care, Urmila."

Urmila was readying to see her off, but by the time she trudged to the front door, Randy called out, "Don't trouble yourself; take rest and see you soon!"

The "soon" dawned in about three months' time, when Urmila resumed going down for walks, sunlight-soaking, and yoga.

# The Coalescing of the Religious Rebels – Marching Towards the Vijaypath Yatra

Urmila bumped into Randy again when she was walking alone in the evening. This time, Randy's bestie was hovering over her like a true comrade. The duo was accompanied by a few other residents. To Urmila, Randy & Co. drew a striking resemblance to "Shri Ram's Vijaypath Yatra," bracing for a *mahayudh.* She would have continued to imagine on the lines of Vaanar Sena, Hanuman, Angad, and Vibhishana in the battalion, had not Randy's boisterous "HELLO" derailed her thought processes.

"Guys, she is Urmila, and she moved into PMS a couple of months ago", Randy introduced Urmila to her battalion. After the "Hi's", "Hellos" and "Welcome to PMS" pleasantries, Randy assumed the leadership position and told the others, "I will fill in Urmila about the latest happenings." The others rambled on while Randy and her bestie hung around, engaging Urmila in small talk and then some serious talk.

Randy briefed Urmila on some developments at the Adcom front and how she had reached out and networked with many residents to initiate the Uprising of 2017. The way she spoke about high 'conversion rates' among residents would have made a seasoned evangelist bow out in shame. All these converts and new recruits (residents) had one thing in common: a skirmish with the Adcom, and they were eager to settle scores with the 'autocrats'. These 'victim' residents coalesced in clusters and in cahoots to form a strategic alliance and overthrow the "Raavan Raj," alias the Adcom.

Thus the "Religious Rebels" came into being, whose prime ideology was to build a framework of governance based on democracy. They kicked off the campaign by fortifying their defences, primarily by enfolding more residents in their camp. Randy's bestie, the veritable 'Amit Shah' being the social butterfly that she was, took up the role of the campaigner, luring the young and old, resident and non-resident owners, veterans and new entrants. The scenario was similar to Lok Sabha elections, with MLAs playing vote bank politics, defecting to other parties, or onboarding unheard-of human entities just for numeric strength.

Rudy, the champion for women's cause, for instance, was recruited for the purpose of growing the "yes man" band in the Religious Rebels group. His spouse was automatically entailed to increase the TRPs of the group through active participation in development and cultural activities (even in the face of turbulence, the entertainment avenues were open to explore, be it Ganesh Chaturthi, Independence Day, Teej Vrat, Onam, etc.). Urmila and Srivatsan were automatically enlisted, for one due to their common ethnicity; secondly, Srivatsan's entertaining WhatsApp rebuttals against the Adcom were the de facto recruiting factor for both husband and wife; and thirdly, Vats' return to India was due in three months' time.

Needless to say, common ethnicity was a binding force among the new members. For instance, the Tamizh attracted the Tamizh, the Malayali, who roped in the other Malayali, so on. The protozoic group thus grew in size to become one large organism that would function with a unified focus—to oust Adcom, primarily. The Religious Rebels' group members who got absorbed into this 'organism' were assigned different roles to ensure the success of the mission: campaigners, double agents, whistle-blowers, and infallible RAW agents.

The classified RAW agents were hand-picked after putting their political allegiance and social equations through the litmus test. The test was to prove sworn animosity to the Adcom plus annulled social equations with those members, or none at all, to start with. This is where Snape pictured himself carrying out his undercover operations. He would plant ingenious bugs and secret devices, tap telephone calls, et al. But he lacked the physical stature of a RAW agent, being lanky and dangling like droopy vines, which would snap at the slightest whiff of the breeze. His lack of physical stature, however, was amply made up for with a mind that outweighed the craftiest politician on earth.

# The Sneaking in of Snape

Snape had first surfaced during one of the fiercest historic WhatsApp wars in PMS. This was with respect to alleged fiscal fudging over bringing in Cauvery water supplies to the apartment. He had piped in with the most provocative remark about the "leader" of the Adcom, adding fuel to the fire and letting it explode to undiminished proportions. It translated to 500+ WhatsApp messages within a span of sixty minutes.

Snape's wily fox behaviour had caught Randy's eye. And before the world knew it, their friendship was forged in cast iron. The future would witness them as partners in crime in many of the misadventures that unfolded in PMS. Snape carried out many 'undercover' missions, with his gadgets waiting in ambush to entrap the 'rogue elements' and catch them red-handed in action.

After the Religious Rebels succeeded in ascending to the throne to form the first MC, Snape got himself elected as a co-opted member. Snape's escapades as an undercover agent riled up many residents in the community. As a mute operator, he would carry out his covert operations and let others step to the forefront to fight the battle or ride the controversy. A classic instance during the tenure of the first MC was the planting of a mobile camera in the Facility Manager's room by Snape.

The mission behind Operation 'Hidden Camera' was to catch the rogue elements of the opposition party red-handed for their unruly behaviour. When the Facility Management office was bombarded and the hidden camera detected by the front runners of the opposition, all hell broke loose. From a volley of complaints about unethical behaviour and violation of privacy to gate-crashing the Facility Management Services' office, the drama that unfolded was akin to Shakespeare's Coriolanus, displaying politics at full scale. The only difference here was that the supporting riotous mob's vitriolic reactions found their way out on WhatsApp, emails, and other social media channels rather than taking action on the ground.

# The Coronation of the Religious Rebels and the Aftermath

Six months later, the Rebels came to power in the year 2018, with barely any opposition. Randy nominated herself for the position of Secretary. Randy's comrade Ritz Carlton (or as Urmila referred to her as Ritz), assumed the VP position. Ritz, as per Randy, matched the Adcom in audacity and aloofness, plus she had the air of one who could run corporate governance on her little pinky. Srivatsan joined the committee as a co-opted member to convey political allegiance to other members of the group. They were hailed as the "Ocean's 11" by the rebels' group, which envisaged them as the pioneering architects of ideal governance in PMS society.

As Urmila reminisced, *Ocean's 11's* initial enthusiasm dissipated into disparate opinions, ideas, and multiple work silos in less than six months. As Srivatsan pointed out once, "There is always a 'nay' rather than an 'ay' to any point of discussion. It makes it challenging to arrive at a consensus." Srivatsan stepped down in a year's time for a lack of bandwidth and on-site participation. Though, as a resident owner, he actively participated in the meetings and raised issues, which, of course, were derisively dismissed. It was one such issue related to financial penalties that made Srivatsan and Randy at loggerheads with each other. The Cold War raged between the MC and the opposition at one end, while on the other, Vats kept insisting on answerability to recurrent issues.

Randy and Ritz became the loudest spokespersons for the committee on all channels of communication, especially WhatsApp. But their loudness did not quell the erstwhile Adcom members, who were seething silently, waiting in ambush for any opportunity to come back at the MC.

Such opportunities came by in plenty, for it soon became evident that there was a lack of cohesion even within the group of 11 committee members. Resolutions to issues were delayed, and the group went incommunicado when demanded for accountability. The teething problems of an incipient society stalled normal functioning. From the STP repair works to overhead tank cleaning, disrupted water supply, swimming pool changing colour, lifts' breakdown, pet poop, and garbage stench that overpowered all the fragrances of PMS, the issues seemed recurrent. More than hard-core brainstorming on the ground to find a solution, all these issues led to an outbreak of epic WhatsApp wars.

The bridges that were burned in the process of the new coalition of the Religious Rebels lay there still giving off smoke. Even the slightest stoking of the 'firewood of the past' led to eruptive episodes, predominantly on WhatsApp.

Randy Raccoon and her compatriot Ritz actively participated in these WhatsApp battles. Their clout gave voice when they noticed their leaders being pushed to the brink of intolerance. As for Urmila, she chose to remain a mute observer. She did not know for sure which side was absolutely in the right or in the wrong. Thus, two years of the primary MC's tenure rolled by, welcoming the year of the pandemic in 2020. For the initial months of the pandemic, panic gripped the community, brushing the political agenda and vendetta beneath the carpet.

Peace reigned, but not for more than a couple of months. The containment and isolation of residents had bottled-up energies of an explosive nature. The WhatsApp clarion blew yet again, with residents being struck with COVID, quarantine, and isolation. The MC's lack of diligence and monitoring came under the radar. By the end of the first wave, it was vastly clear that the primary MC had not created many waves in the way of milestone developments or progress. Routine maintenance was staggering. What brought the lacuna in their processes to the forefront was the recurrent STP water issues. It seemed like the drainpipes of PMS had decided to regurgitate, crying out loud, "Poop for poop, pee for pee." With the sanitisation fever on the rise alongside COVID, the panic-stricken residents took to WhatsApp yet again to break the silence of the ruling party. The common groups were plastered with photos of toilets submerged in untreated STP water. It was like PMS was floating in its underbelly waste!

Urmila's apartment did not face the brunt of overflowing STP water, but the stench had percolated to all the rooms in her house. It was like being compelled to use an oxygen cylinder inside the house itself, though she did make do with a mask, which she wore at all times, till the issue got resolved.

On the one hand, the national media was rife with news about N95 masks, the virus, COVID statistics, and deaths, while the PMS social media (WhatsApp) was overflowing with pictures galore of people's flush talks and their bathroom commodes. What stole the spotlight was the juicy remark from one of the residents, which said, "*Ghar ban gaya shauchalaya*!" "MC should step down from its pedestal to understand the plight of the *aam aadmi*." All the messages conveyed one thing in common: to disallow the current members from continuing to the next tenure. "Quit PMS Association" rang loud. The avalanche of angst among residents came down hard on the MC. But of course, they chose not to respond on WhatsApp, as per their resolve to not use the channel for official communication. It seemed rightfully so, considering the explosive episodes of the past did not yield any output but left residents embittered (But the MC constituted by the Religious Rebels came to terms with the stark realisation that they were not the 'public's favourite. And when the time came for them to step down and hand over, they did while ensuring to hand-pick their God children – Snape, Rudy, the "She" and four others who would continue their lineage for the next tenure. Vats and one other resident were the only non-aligned members in the new formation).

Through these proceedings, Urmila did discover a quintessential element about WhatsApp (or other online media, for that matter). It did not establish LoC or LAC while enabling its users. From name-calling to mudslinging, the offence and defence by the warring parties were carried out with a virtual shield that was as pervasive as a virus that lurks in the atmosphere.

# Do Good LoCs make good Neighbours? – Living in the age of WhatsApp, Instagram, and ChatGPT

Once upon a time, before gated communities sprawled across the urban precincts, residential complexes did not sport high-storeyed buildings. Apartments were not sky-high and touristy to make the neck crane up in wonder. The concept of penthouses or high-floor balconies giving a panoramic view of the city was not in vogue. Next-door neighbours did not live behind closed doors, rather they were found hob-nobbing with their *padosi for* most of the day. The social tenets were based on human connection that came naturally as part of community living. Societies thrived and lived in harmony even in those small complexes, sans the infinity pools of luxury or fancy status symbols such as SUVs, Apple phones, or Bluetooth. People in those days lived in 'open spaces' despite the four walls of their homes, which ensured privacy. They opened up their doors and hearts to their neighbours, who eventually became a part of their extended family.

But it was vastly different now when it came to apartment living, among many other things, as Urmila had discovered in her two-decade-long residency in many gated communities.

After attending to the BLINKIT delivery fellow, Urmila locked her front door shut. She had loads of chores lined up, but that did not restrain her from walking down the memory lane of her childhood days. Her family had spent most of their lives living in an apartment system. But apartments in those days were not built on the lines of a "Lego-land kind of layout." She vividly recalled how her mom or the aunty next-door would walk in, anytime, into each other's homes, just for chitchat or for exchanging homemade goodies. There was nothing to hold them back. Neither were they preoccupied to such an extent as to not be able to make room for a neighbour. A wave of nostalgia swept through Urmila; the yearning for the good old days was compounded with a feeling of emptiness. It is not that she had a dearth of friends or acquaintances in her present apartment. But that feeling of bonding with a neighbour or friend had become hard-wired with prefixed protocols. A neighbourly visit was predefined along the lines of making a doctor's appointment. First, check for free slots, then ping through WhatsApp prior to making the actual visit. If WhatsApp did not evoke a response, the thumb rule was to confirm availability from Instagram to double-confirm the current coordinates of the buddy cum neighbour, as people were readily online and at different spaces for feeding their Instagram reels rather than actually being physically present in their homes.

Instagram seemed like an instant way to connect with the neighbour, who would be hardly ten steps away from your home. WhatsApp had overridden the necessity of physical visits when a message in chat lingo with a wide array of emoticons had been deemed close-to-human contact. What was missing alone, as Urmila mulled over, was the human touch and other sensory perceptions in the entire gamut of online interfaces. It was a virtual world where the boundaries thinned in terms of access and reach. But it had also ensconced people into bubbles, where there was a greater sense of security and insulation against the unsavoury external elements. For instance, let Tower 2 of the apartment be reeling under a power crisis, but it is not a wake-up call for others until it pinches them. Two residents getting into a verbal spat or brawl get the cheering and booing only from their respective clouts. The neutral parties continue to hibernate until they realise that the risk of breaking their glass walls to smithereens runs high.

Urmila stepped out to her balcony, facing the IT park, which spreadeagled to the horizon. The glass-walled buildings refracted myriad images of the residential blocks in the vicinity. It seemed that the human settlement was an encroachment on the enclave of technology. These glasshouses were wired in and connected, and the loose ends of those wires had crept into the lives of every human on earth, raising mini glass-walled living spaces. So, 'connected yet out of touch', was the new-age mantra for community living.

The added advantage of online connections like WhatsApp was, of course, the virtual IDs, which made it difficult to differentiate between humans and bots. These chat channels also enabled and empowered a heretofore repressed demon within every human and brought it to light. Much like a gaming app, where avatars could be created, WhatsApp enabled the "split personality" of those who could bring out their repressed personas and lead a double life in the virtual mode, undetected. The timid could become a superhero, the shy could become outspoken, the thief could become the police, or the silent protestor could turn into a vociferous torchbearer.

"C'mon, all humans have a dark side, Mom." her high school daughter once remarked, not so long ago, while the mom-daughter duo was having heated discussions about the ills of social media. Her daughter was not wrong. The flurry of antagonistic messages against the MC or going ballistic at the drop of a hat on WhatsApp on many occasions did raise many questions: whether the civilised members of PMS had secret WhatsApp avatars carved out of the Amazon wild? Was the virtual world actually unleashing the dark forces of nature?

Urmila felt the darkness enveloping her, with no sight of reprieve for Srivatsan from the current crisis. She could not stomach it any longer, and desperately needed a confidant who would listen to her tales of woe. So, Urmila decided to brush aside all new-age protocols of neighbourliness and ring the doorbell of her neighbour, Meenu. Though recently moved in, Urmila's next-door neighbour Meenakshi or "Meenu" was affable, and the two neighbours struck an instant rapport with each other.

Meenu had exuded so much warmth even on the first day of their meeting that Urmila did not find the need for any more icebreakers to just drop by her next-door neighbour for a friendly chat.

# *Aamney-Samney* – Crossing over LoC's, Without Being an Infiltrator

Urmila was at the doorstep of Meenu's and pressed the doorbell switch a little pensively. Meenu opened the door with the most ebullient "Hiiiiii!"

"What a pleasant surprise, Urmi. Come in, come in."

"Hey Meenu, I hope I am not barging in. You weren't busy with anything, that I am disturbing you?" Urmila spoke in a hesitant voice.

"Arrey, c'mon, yaar. YOU ARE NOT BEING A disturbance! I will feel offended if you continue talking like this", Meenu tapped Urmila's shoulder chidingly.

"Ok, ok, I won't. Chill." Urmila responded, looking at the changed artwork in Meenu's drawing room. She settled down on the couch.

"Mridula has an amazing artistic streak, doesn't she?" Urmila could not stop admiring the abstract art done by Meenu's daughter, Mridula. Most of Mridula's artwork was on display in Meenu's living room. Looking at those abstract arts kind of diffused Urmila's current stressful situation. She felt that the colours and shades and the figure sketches hidden in them absorbed the chaos of her world. Like dancers who find rhythm in absolute noise, Urmila sought solace in the space she was in, now.

Meenu, on the other hand, was brewing a fresh cuppa in the kitchen. Urmila had forgotten that she had come in, just in time for tea. Meenu called out from the kitchen, "Urmi, how much, *cheeni?*" "Only a spoon, not more, Meenu." Urmila continued her drift towards the art display, soaking it all. Before she knew, what conjured up before Urmila's eyes was not just *garam garam chai* but a snack platter to go with it. Meenu was laying everything on the teapoy while asking Urmila to help herself.

"Dig right in, Urmi! These biscuits are Mumbai special!", Meenu gestured towards the snack platter.

Urmila could not resist either the aromas or the visual appeal of what was laid before her. She picked up a couple of biscuits while sipping her tea. "This tea tastes heavenly, Meenu! It is so refreshing!"

"Glad you are enjoying it. So, how has it been with you? It has been so long." Meenu settled down on the couch opposite to Urmila.

"All is ok, I guess. It has been the usual with kids and their busy schedules. I haven't had time for myself yet. It has been ages since I went down for a walk! How has it been for you?"

"You know, Urmi, I am hardly here. There has been so much on my itinerary that "HOME" comes in as the last place to visit on my list! But it was good catching up with my buddies in Mumbai. The BFF kind of meets!"

"That is great, Meenu! I wish I could squeeze out a breather to catch up with my old timers! By the way, is anything planned for the Diwali celebration? You are part of that group, correct?"

"Honestly, since I am hardly in PMS, I seldom get to catch up with those folks. I only tele-talk to be in touch or

WhatsApp in the group. That reminds me, what was the latest furore in the groups about loud music coming from Tower 2?"

"Who knows, Meenu? There could have been some bachelor's parties in full swing! Or, for all you know, it could have been just music played with speakers on; that would have peeved the neighbour! I mean, there is no saying where to mark the fences to be a good neighbour these days!"

Urmila continued, "You wouldn't believe the things that had happened here much before you moved in. A few residents from the same floor were involved in "territory disputes." The 4-series flats claim that they are entitled to a greater area in the corridor as they pay more maintenance. The complaint from the neighbour was about the garbage bin being kept at the far end of their corridor, leading to a stench on the entire floor. The disputing residents sought the intervention of the MC to mark their boundaries. The ruling that was enforced with respect to the garbage bins was to keep the bin close to your doorway. Not to keep your trash anywhere near the common area."

"Seriously, Urmi? I understand we need to respect privacy and not be a neighbourly nuisance. But hype and hoopla for everything show heights of intolerance! On top of that, everybody is a self-proclaimed authority on any subject. Information is either googled up or simply sourced from the likes of CHAT GPT."

"True, Meenu. Sometimes, because of the way it is scripted to underlie the tone of subject expertise, I feel the text is copy-pasted from CHAT GPT. Looking back at it, it is surprising how we survived the pandemic, especially the first wave! There was chaos and the false spreading of information. People were going paranoid. Any affected flat or resident would face a barrage of queries—when were the first symptoms detected? Did you use the lift or step out when you had the first symptoms, etc.? I mean, I get that everybody at that time wanted to stay safe. But there is a humane approach to such sensitive issues. Just because some residents are affected, you can't treat them as a social pariah in society. By asking insensitive queries in the WhatsApp groups or ratting out about their flouting COVID norms, the list is endless. Of course, there was the volunteer group that ensured some degree of sanity in society by being proactive about the quarantined, ensuring prompt notifications, and reaching out for their daily needs (groceries, medicines, cooked food if needed)."

Meenu nodded in assent. "I have noticed so many messages in WhatsApp groups about apartment issues. The language used is unwelcome. I mean, yes, stopping the water supply without notice or making abrupt power cuts is not welcome. But there is a way to communicate it. People just go berserk on WhatsApp, not knowing where to draw the line!"

"Tell me about it! There was this hilarious, infuriating WhatsApp *mahayudh*. It involved Vats when he was in the MC. Some residents had recorded an adolescent boy going topless in the gym and shared it with one of the MC members. Vats was asked to discuss it one-on-one with the resident (the father) concerned. The father got offended and shared the video in the owners' WhatsApp group. One thing led to another about violations of privacy and all sorts. However, the focus on the issue was lost, with numerous tangents regarding common rules in the discussion thread. The highlight was the raging battle between Vats and one lady of the group. Mind you, she was in no way related to the photographed boy.

"Imagine Meenu, how this WhatsApp war would have raged like Mahabharata II", Urmila spoke while trying to show that discussion to Meenu for entertainment purposes. She had earmarked those 7-D cinema-scale messages for posterity. But while scrolling through her WhatsApp groups, she saw a message pop up from an unknown number.

The message read, "Poor you. With what Srivatsan has done, you guys need to visit a marriage counsellor. It might help you both to see the truth. Being a woman, you should stand up for women's rights and voice against what your husband has done."

Urmila had turned pale; her brow puckered when she was reading and re-reading the message. Meenu noticed the sudden change in Urmila's expression: "Urmi, is everything all right?"

"Ya, ya," Urmila spoke in haste as she got up to leave. "I just remembered something. So, I better get going."

She strode towards the door and looked in askance, "And hey, Meenu, thanks for everything!"

"Anytime, Urmi. Take care."

# Women's Rights – The Shakti Caught 'tween Misguided Feminism & Misinterpreted Empowerment

Urmila turned on her laptop and logged into WhatsApp Web to trace the unknown number who had sent the message. She scoured all the residents' groups she was part of but could not map the number to any of the members of those groups. This definitely seemed to be the case with the double identity and split personality personas of WhatsApp.

Her immediate reaction was to call up Srivatsan. But he was at the office, and his schedule had been busy because of the financial year-end audit. So, she decided to leave it for the day to catch up after he returned home.

But the 'howler' message left her seething in fury. She curbed her instincts to barge into the Facility Management office and confront the two ladies, who were the cause of Srivatsan's imbroglio. The message conveyed one thing clearly. The unauthorised recordings by Snape that were used against Vats as evidence was now being circulated in the MC group's social circle. This could not have been the doing of any MC member, as it risked exposure and dishonour for an official bearer by getting his hands dirty. One of the 'foot soldiers' in their camp, with no sense of morality or sensibility, must have been deployed for this task.

"The audacity of the messenger!", Urmila muttered through clenched teeth.

"Ah, being a woman, the message says! What would these pompous goons know about fighting for women's causes or their rights? Urmila thought loudly.

Urmila was long associated with NGOs to support victims of abuse and harassment. Some of these NGOs were tied up with corporates to provide to employees as well, both men and women. Studying the rising incidence of cases, where men were wrongly implicated, was a revelation to Urmila. As per government mandates, corporates had devised schemas to give women more latitude to report cases of abuse or harassment. None of the provisions in the law factored in the incidence of entrapment, "favours" or luring by women. All that was given weight was the word of the woman in such cases. Stories of entrapment by women, which left their male counterparts with sabotaged careers, family disgrace, and lost means of livelihood, showed staggering statistics. But such stories seldom made front-page news.

Through her engagement with campaigns on women's cause, Urmila observed that feminism outweighed the true empowerment of women. Feminism stood out as an iconoclast in a system of patriarchy. It had managed to build a glamour quotient for itself, entailing more of the privileged women on its bandwagon, thereby benefiting them more. The feminist ideologies, at most times, preached rebellion and retaliation rather than finding a solution that would address the problem at its grassroots.

The problem of society was the patriarchy-entrenched male mindset, the domestically submissive female adaptation to the environment, and the myth and misconception that women are sculpted out of *Ashok Van's* Sita, the character from Hindu mythology (Rama's wife from the great Indian epic Ramayana who is kept hostage in the forest of the demon king, Lanka. She pines for her husband throughout her period of stay in Lanka). The universal truth that holds good to date is that men are not biologically wired to act like *'Maryaada Purshottam' as* personified by Lord Ram, who is pledged to not look beyond his wife, Sita (observing the vows of the *Ekpatnivrata*). That does not justify infidelity or domestic abuse. But it explains why men are not conditioned to resist luring or being tempted easily. This weakness of men is strung to the feminine guiles, which brand women as vile seductresses.

Women's empowerment aims at breaking these cliches associated with women. Urmila had brought out these aspects in many of the women-centric workshops and seminars she had hosted. She firmly believed that true woman prowess lay in self-sustainability, self-worth, and self-belief. She would argue with no restraint on public forums that the true manifestation of Shakti in every woman happens only when women play by their strengths and not weaknesses. The "weaker" sex remains "weak" if they continue using their viles and guiles to entrap men, just for the whim of it.

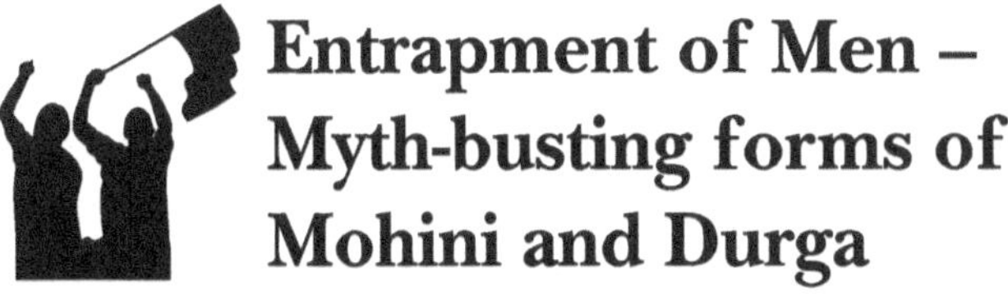

# Entrapment of Men – Myth-busting forms of Mohini and Durga

As an avid listener of stories of mythology, Urmila recalled how her grandmother would eulogise the prowess of Durga or Kali. To Urmila's impressionable, young mind, these goddesses assumed the superhero stature, all braced up to wipe out the evil off the earth. It was much later in life that, while expounding the depth of these stories for work-related projects, she learned that Durga or Kali manifested only to quash the demonic male ego (be it Mahishasur or Raktbheej).

"Tinkling laughter with the jingling of anklets filled the air." Urmila could hear her grandmother's accompanying sound effects rendered for Mohini while narrating about the ten avatars of Vishnu, which had taken a turn towards the beautiful feminine avatar of Lord Vishnu.

"She batted her eyelids, and her dimpled smile was enough to cast a spell on the Asuras. All their years of fatigue from churning the ocean for the *Amrut* (celestial ambrosia, the nectar of immortality) vanished into thin air. For what stood before them was a celestial maiden of unparalleled beauty. She was none other than Vishnu, who had assumed this beautiful form to entice the asuras and the *Amrutha Kalasha* from their hands. The asuras consuming the *Amrutha* would spell destruction for the three worlds. So, Mohini was the answer to the prayers of the Devas, who had approached Lord Vishnu to trick the asuras and snatch the ambrosia without fuss. Enchanting the asuras with her beauty, Mohini succeeds in snatching the nectar from their hands." Grandma would enact this part in a classic way with a wry smile, crowning her triumphant look.

It was this look that came flashing back to Urmila. That was the shadow of a smirk writ on the faces of the two ladies who were responsible for framing Srivatsan. They were no 'Mohinis' or celestial nymphs by any textbook standards. And Srivatsan was not any demon for such a clash between male and feminine forces to have erupted.

Yet, here, the battle was raging to no end. The fact that Lady 1, whom Urmila had given the misnomer 'Slime', had volunteered information about her personal problems and later blamed Srivatsan for trying to intimidate her for 'favours' was infuriating to no end. The real-life exchanges between Vats and Slime kept playing back in her mind, especially the excerpt where Slime had pulled off a great show as a damsel in distress.

"With what confidence are you telling me your personal things?" asked Vats in his usual upfront manner.

"I believe in you, sir. I like you. That is why I am comfortable telling you these things." Slime had said in reply.

The subsequent communication on WhatsApp about frequent hospitalisation due to her menstrual problems was testimony to the truth that Slime had sought Vats' counsel.

Rather, as Urmila figured out later, Slime wanted to conveniently excuse herself from the daily duties by seeking a pity party from Vats. And this 'seeking' bordered on flirtation. Why Vats alone? The decisive conclusion Urmila could arrive at was that Vats was the only MC member who was behind their backs to get the work done properly. It was natural that they had to 'placate the boss' till the tenure of the then-ruling MC came to an end. But when Slime got to know that Vats had nominated himself for the next MC, she joined hands with her partner in crime (whom Urmila gave the moniker 'Parashakti') to frame Vats. But the partners in crime would not have succeeded in pulling off their act without Snape's unflinching support.

Urmila had reiterated this to her husband: "Vats, don't you think that Snape had colluded with the Facility Management? Slime could be Snape's pawn, for all you know!"

Vats had given Urmila's viewpoint the benefit of the doubt: "I have seen him in the FM office on a daily basis. Of course, he has doled out special boxes of sweets to Slime for his daughter's birthday. Give it to the entire staff; that is understandable. But, to her alone, that was unnecessary. What irked me was the fact that Slime does not have proper credentials for Indian citizenship; she has a Dubai address. Snape was supposed to be involved in the background checks. Talk about professionalism, and look who is not walking the talk! "With this guy, anything is possible!", Vats sounded like an ominous Oracle declaring that a monstrous rogue had run amok!

Urmila could only desperately pray that Vats was wrong, and Snape did not wield the last word on the larger clout of patrons and followers who had hand-picked him to continue their regime. This was no less than dynasty politics by the national parties of the country, which had raised contentions amongst the opposition. Dynasty politics and mafia rule had come to be in PMS society. Urmila feared that the 30-odd residents, who represented the majority for critical decisions and resolutions, constituted the clout of Snape, along with Randy Raccoon, Ritz, Rudy, and their chain of contacts in the society. Randy Raccoon led this group. Urmila was sure that it was one of Randy's group members who would have sent her that anonymous message. "That slimy, bitchin' sow!", Urmila could swear to her heart's content with the choicest of expletives, as she was not within earshot of a single human, primarily her kids.

She felt the rage bubbling inside her, like a volcano. For an instant, she wondered whether she would morph into a goddess with eight limbs, just like the MTR ads featuring a multi-tasking homemaker. But instead of wielding delectable delicacies, as in the ad, she would wield weapons of choice to wipe out Randy's clout by exposing their evil doings. And stomp over their remains with a victory dance. But she had to rein herself in. The social influence had to be penetrated, not with violence but with diplomacy. Urmila tucked in her newly-fangled, fierce form and opened the MS Word document on her laptop instead. She sketched a map of the social influencers of PMS and gave them fancy names and even more fanciful honours while assessing their sphere of influence in the society.

# Of Meerkats & Queen Bees – Navigating the Sphere of Social Influence in Community Living

Apart from Randy Raccoon's, other cliques of prominence existed in PMS. For instance, the ones who were followers of the Fantastic Four. Then, there were the fitness freaks who measured their steps by the minute, stretched their walking regimen to yoga, and ran the gossip mill with unlimited fodder (with fact files and stories comparable to Indian soaps). The chieftains of these cliques stood on par with each other. They were power-puffed with news and information that was capable of sparking off a global-scale forest fire or even giving journalists a run for their money.

Neither Urmila nor Srivatsan were aligned with any of the cliques. Urmila was not a social butterfly by nature, and she preferred to keep a safe distance while maintaining the basic social equation of cordiality. The ladies' coterie of PMS were social influencers with a distinct following. As popular and notorious as they were, they kept PMS vibrant and downcast at the same time. Their misguided zeal knew no bounds. The ladies of these cliques ensured that the 'grapevines of PMS' yielded both sweet and sour grapes. Most of the residents in the close-knit or far-reaching network of these groups feasted on the harvest of these vines, as long as the seeds were not stolen from their garden. 'Talk about what '*Rasaleela*' is happening in another's house; I will enjoy the laugh riot to no end!' was their motto.

Urmila had by now identified the active members of these cliques as

- Meerkats: To be tuned to the slightest whiff of randy-ish gossip, extricate the matter from the deepest (even if it is the netherworld) recesses and keep the respective clique as a prime-time news forum.
- Queen Bees: To delegate and outsource the errands for the drones in the group. Collecting the 'nectar' of spicy scoops from other cliques, islands of solitary residents, and the worker class in the Facility Management team

If one were to witness the Amazon wild in action, the meerkats would steal the show as a cohesive social group. Perking their ears up at the slightest disturbance in their environment, the meerkats could always be counted upon to pick on anything within their radar of hearing and sight. The queen bees, on the other hand, could be compared to the lazy leader of a group who would delegate work to the underlings while slopping on a tree branch for sun-basking and sipping cocktails.

These instincts undoubtedly aided in survival in the wild, and they did not vanish into thin air with humans coming to settle as civilisations. Higher in the evolutionary tree, the brain added layers of complexity to these instincts. Just like packaging raw beans and carrots in a zesty, complex dish, the brain of the homo sapiens honed 'basic instincts' in an octopus-like package whose tentacles entwined the most indecipherable of human behaviour.

Human ancestors from the animal kingdom, namely the chimpanzees and apes, have been studied closely to trace the lineage of many mysterious human qualities. Their troops engage in chatter and mockery, mark the outliers, and banish the outcaste, not to mention they also demonstrate empathy and compassion within a troop. What catches the eye even in the kingdom of apes is the fight for dominance to be the alpha male or the coveted female. The legacy of the dominant gene has been passed on through generations of humans with myriad manifestations. From the kings to the Vikings to the leaders and modern-day social media influencers, Indian and American idols are worshipped with the religious fervour shown to a god or guru. The following and the followers of these influencers, though invisible, can be compared to the crowd-pulling effects of the MahaKumbh mela.

Likewise, the social influencers in the PMS apartment complex had their fair share of followers, who could be classified as 'Blind Bhakts'. They had the power to make or break the reputation of any individual in society. The classic case was that of the Fantastic Four, whose reputation was brought to ruins, thanks to Randy Raccoon's newly burgeoning clique at that time. Similarly, Fitness Freaks had a wide sphere of influence as they were the top-notch meerkats of society. From a 5-year-old to a 50-year-old, none could escape the cynosure of the Fitness Freaks' eyes.

The Queen Bee of this group once mentioned to Urmila, while meeting her down, "You don't have to walk at all. You are already so thin. Have you ever thought of eating ghee *laddoos* on a daily basis?"

Urmila just laughed off, saying, "Oh no, I don't want to morph into a laddoo! Then I would be rolling on the ground here. I will not be able to race you guys at all."

They parted ways, but before Urmila could get out of earshot, she could hear Queen Bee and her buddies giggling and commenting about the dress sense of the teen girls who had just passed by them. " I think we should tell her mother about letting her daughter wear such teensy clothes. She is not a 5-year-old anymore." The active respondent in the group replied, "What if her mother allows her to wear such clothes?" Queen Bee piped in with the most juicy remark: "She is part of my other kitty group. A glass of Bacardi instead of routine chai will make her see why young girls should be raised *sanskaari.*"

Not just teens, but their own peer group were not off the radar either. Paunches were grossly mistaken for buds in the oven. Once a religious solitary walker was taken by surprise when one of Queen Bee's followers waylaid her to say, "You kept it a secret, huh? When is the good news going to be delivered?" The much-taken-aback solitary walker replied, "No, no, I am under hormone treatment. No good news, only a good expanding tummy!"

The main fodder for the gossip mill of these cliques was fed by the ruling MC and their unfair rules, or about high-charging maids, overbearing in-laws, or conspicuously visible live-ins who wandered in the apartment with no sense of shame. The "hi-tea crones" (men and women exclusively) group kept themselves entertained with hi-tea huddles in the clubhouse or the gazebos. What the huddles constituted was not much to wonder about, as the elderly mothers and mothers-in-law would talk of cooking while cooking up spicy stuff about their irreverent *bahus.* Not to mention, they actively participated in the apartment culturals as well.

"What would the social influencers have to say once the word spreads about the expulsion of Vats from the committee? Will they take in the word of Snape and his clout at face value? Or, is there even a remote possibility that there will be an amicable resolution before this issue is dragged to the GBM, which was due soon?" These questions bombarded Urmila like pincers poking into an open wound. She was worried to death about the repercussions, more so about their social image. The Queen Bees and Meerkats would leave no stone unturned to exaggerate the reality. Randy Raccoon, for one, will not think twice about letting loose the Twitter of gossip, which would undoubtedly rage like the cry of a hyena successful in a scavenger hunt. Urmila bit her lips hard as she received notifications about apna complex notices for the GBM. The agenda had changed once again with the addendum, "Reason for not considering certain nominations."

What lay in store for Urmila and Srivatsan in the upcoming GBM? What twist of fate awaited them? They could only bid their time.

Residents Association - From Welfare to Warfare, when Women's Rights become Weapons of character Assassination

# The Fateful GBM – A Week Before the Ides of March 2023

"Beware of the Ides of March"; the soothsayer had warned Julius Caesar about his impending doom. Urmila could feel it in her gut. March 8 will drag Vats' name to the gutters. Swords will be drawn to pierce through the family's honour and dignity. Urmila knew that Snape, Rudy, and the "She" (the 'Tricking Trio', as Urmila started referring to them)' would stoop to any level to justify their stand on expelling Vats. The countdown began, with just 5 days to go. And neither Urmila nor Vats wanted the issue of expulsion to be dragged into the owners' meeting. At the same time, Vats was not ready to initiate any kind of meeting with the MC members, especially the Tricking Trio—the "She", Rudy, and Snape.

But Vats was very clear on one thing: the withdrawal of all notices against him by the MC and the Facility Management company through writing. As explained by his advocate, every notice had to be produced in writing with authorised signatories. Vats had explained to Urmila, "Since they are so keen on my not continuing in the next MC, I have to push for getting these notices withdrawn. On one side, I submit my resignation, the other side they withdraw the notice. It happens in parallel. That is how it should go."

Urmila bit her lip, a visible frown writ on her face. "I hope it does not get dragged to the GBM, Vats."

Vats was looking at his phone and headed towards the door. He looked back at Urmila and said, "Rishi wants to have a meeting at the clubhouse. Let's see what he has to say."

Vats had been coordinating with the Election Officer, Rishi, who was ratifying the nominations for the new MC. Also, with his role came the unpleasant job of being a peacemaker between the warring parties. He was the conduit between Vats and the MC members who were pitching for Vats' resignation.

Urmila had nicknamed the EO "POP," or the Puppet of Pleasers, as he would recede into oblivion whenever it came to dealing with the issue head-on. He would emerge as the veritable peacemaker in WhatsApp discussions. In the guise of finesse, his ambiguity came out uncamouflaged. In short, because of this very nature of his, he was a successful fringe player as part of the many socio-political factions of PMS.

On the issue related to Vats, POP maintained the stoic silence of the Buddha, trying to absorb everything. Knowing his wishy-washy tendencies, Urmila lashed out angrily, "He is fit for nothing. Instead of trying to be atmospheric about this whole issue and taking a strong stand, he is only taking the viewpoints presented to him by Snape." Urmila continued, "Shouldn't he be more neutral in his approach to this crisis? All I can say is that they have all ganged up."

Vats gave a slight nod of agreement and headed towards the front door. Urmila cried out before he could close the door. "Be careful about what you say to him, Vats. You can't trust him either!"

Half an hour later, Vats returned. Urmila could barely wait for him to settle down. With bated breath, she asked him, "What did Rishi say? Are they ready to give it in writing?"

"Nope, what they propose is this: they will delete the emails and other data related to this from the record. But nothing will be given in writing." Vats spoke resignedly. "Don't worry, Urmi. Let us see what happens. The more we cower before them, the more they will try to crush us. I have not done anything wrong. If we don't get a resolution here, let the law take its course."

# The Curtain Rises on the GBM of 8/03/2023 – Judgement Day

The shafts of the afternoon sun seeped through their bedroom window as Urmila and Vats were peeking through it. It gave them a good view of the front side of their apartment, along the pathway that led to the clubhouse.

They could see the residents walking towards the clubhouse for the GBM. Most of them were recognisable because of their characteristic gait. Randy Raccoon, Ritz, and Rudy with projectors and sorts. The mentors of the current MC could be seen marching towards the clubhouse. Among them were a few tenants as well, whom Vats had interacted with in the past.

"Vats, look, even Prateek is heading towards the clubhouse. Tenants can be proxies for their owners, correct?" Prateek was a long-time tenant in Urmila's tower, part of the sportsmen clique in PMS, comprising many resident owners. He was an active protestor of Snape's regime, as mooted by his comrades in the sports group.

"Yes. Come, let us also go to the GBM and see what they have to say."

Both Urmila and Srivatsan started towards the clubhouse. The moment they reached the doorway of the party hall where the meeting was to take place, they noticed the frontline of seats was occupied by the Meerkats of PMS. Randy Raccoon was the first among them, who alerted the others huddling with her.

The entrance of Srivatsan and Urmila into the room had a dramatic effect. One by one, the heads popped up, like meerkats disturbed from their huddles in the wild Amazon who got wind of a prey or predator in their territory. Urmila was reminded of the classic scene from the Lion King movie when the gathered wild animals of Pride Rock stomp and boo in outrage at the traitor animal, who brings disgrace to Pride Rock. Urmila thought, "Who is the traitor here?"

After everybody settled down, POP briefed the group about the agenda. The last addendum to the agenda was the expulsion of Srivatsan. It was at this juncture that the "She" pitched in. While getting up from her seat, she callously dropped her mobile on the same chair and let out a deep sigh. As Urmila could see from the seat right behind her, the "She" assumed the air of one who had been called to deal with the dregs of society. Much like a queen who would rather inspect the polish on the gems of her throne than step down from it to deal with stolen jewels from the kingdom. The "She" however, carried her attitude forward and spoke like the "Oracle". Beside her, like a tech prop, was Rudy with projectors, a laptop, and so on. Her opening lines were, "It had come to our notice from the Facility Management lady staff that one of the MC members..." Throughout her narrative, she referred to Srivatsan as "the accused", who had refused to comply with the protocols, the majority's decision to expel him, and his denial of the accusations despite the recordings.

A few residents interjected, "Who is that member? We want to know who he is." Another resident, like a Gyan

Guru, piped in, "We don't tolerate such behaviour in corporates. Why should we tolerate it here?"

The "She" nodded vigorously in assent. "That is what we told him. We had seven meetings with the accused, just to convince him to step down."

"We are living in the midst of a S*X PREDATOR. Why aren't we reporting to the police?", A grating voice came from behind the room. Urmila turned to look back at the owner of the voice. The resident had once collaborated with Vats for some business. Urmila held Vats' hand, clenching it tightly, to dissipate her anger. Both she and Vats had agreed before coming to the meeting that they would not give room for any outburst. What made it even more difficult for Urmila to contain herself was when the "She" made a scathing remark, "I too am afraid to even step out with such people living in our community."

Urmila was appalled and disgusted to hear Srivatsan being spoken about in such a manner. For somebody who had tirelessly worked day and night for society, such insults being hurtled at was not one bit acceptable. She had to exercise considerable restraint, as she was seething like the "HULK," eager to smash the people and premise of the forum.

To prevent the meeting from turning into a big fight, Ritz, who was standing right behind in the room, cut short the "She's" rhetoric, stating, "Let us focus on the main agenda of the meeting and move forward."

The "She" took the cue and requested a vote of hands in favour of the resolution. Hands went up, and, in some cases, two hands from the same person went up to show up for a proxy. Both Urmila and Srivatsan noticed the overt overzealousness in a few residents, favouring the resolution. These were primarily the founding members of the "Religious Rebels" group.

It was clear that the splinter group of the Rebels had treated Vats as an outlier from the beginning. The fact that they could not exact political allegiance from him and make him collude with their policies, without question, frustrated them. And blowing this issue out of proportion and levying such charges on Vats paved the way for his quick exit. At least that is what they assumed.

The vote of hands and the decisive conclusion to expel Vats were followed by a loud murmur. "Who is it? Why can't you tell his name?" "We have to consider the family before we reveal such things in public," the "she" had responded.

Urmila and Srivatsan got up just then to find the exit route from the meeting. After coming out of the clubhouse, Urmila noticed that the FM was stationed at the reception of the clubhouse. Urmila spoke to Srivatsan from between clenched teeth: "We were not even given a chance to speak. Even a death row inmate is given a chance to speak. You have worked as their core team member, been there to ensure smooth maintenance, and pitched in for every crisis. This is utterly uncivilised, diabolical, and vindictive! Snape will pay for this one day!"

"Urmi, calm down. They would not have expected our presence. If they had even one bit of common sense, they would have understood that the ones who are guilty do not come out in the open." Vats continued, "They are visibly angry, as I did not yield to their pressure! Since they did not give me a chance to justify my side, I will have to address the owners' forum through mail."

That night saw Srivatsan draft a four-page email, rendering the context and background of the entire episode of "messages", "harassment" and "accusations." Urmila felt deeply pained for her husband having to go through this but was helpless to do anything about it.

What struck her as weird was that just a week prior to the eruption of this episode (February 28), both Snape and the "She" direly sought Vats' involvement in a highly sensitive incident on the premises; it involved an adolescent girl, and the matter had to be brought to the attention of her mother. At that time, Vats was deemed 'ideal' to deal with a woman's issue. And now…

As Vats clicked the "Send" button on his mail, Urmila sat beside him on the couch. The gentle breeze seeping in from the gaps of the French windows in the living room seemed to tug at the oil painting on the wall, right above the couch. It was modern abstract art with a hazy depiction of buildings, juxtaposed between light and dark. The painting caught her eye, and looking at it intently, Urmila could visualise the entire picture fitting into her current mental frame. The painting looked like an abstract of gated communities, with a diversity of individuals disparate in their own islands.

# Of Misadventures, Murky Waters and Merriment – Minding the M's and C's and the in-between

As the picture frame tapped gently against the wall, Urmila could see the entities in the painting coming to life.

The buildings overlooked the walkways, lit by dim streetlights. Urmila noticed the solitary man on the sidewalk bench, with his hatchet alone to give him company. Random people could be seen huddling around the cafeteria across the roads. Not to mention the stray dog, sniffing for a bite or two from the throwaway box; a canoodling couple in a shady corner; and a seedy-looking man with a top hat leaning against the wall. Two glasses of wine could be seen sparkling on the tabletop that protruded from the window sill of one of these buildings. Running alongside the window sills were clotheslines pegged up with underpants and napkins. They seemed to flutter like prayer flags in the mountain breeze. Urmila could feel the tug of the breeze gambolling with her loose hair strands and, at the same time, swaying the balance of the wine glass along the window sill. It tipped and went crashing down the many stories of the building, just as the glass that was kept by her feet went rolling down the floor when she turned more towards the painting.

The sound of glass breaking to smithereens brought back flashing memories of whisky bottles being flung from the windows of upper-storeyed flats in PMS. The incident had created a furore on WhatsApp and also on the ground, as it had become an evening ritual of a tipsy resident, who seemed to be living his life on the lines of a *Sharaabi,* emulating the mega-cinema star Amitabh Bacchan. But unlike Amitabh, the '*Sharaabi*' of PMS seemed to refrain from vocalising his sorrows, for he did not serenade from his balcony or by his window side while flinging his bottle! As part of the MC, Vats was actively involved in catching the culprit, as the preceding incident reported was about bottle-flinging into the kids' play zone. He went door-to-door with a few ladies whose kids had apparently witnessed the incident. No degree of interrogation brought anything to the fore. However, the MC decided to station security personnel at the vantage points around Tower 2 for additional vigilance. Eventually, the mysterious *Sharaabi* fizzled out into oblivion, along with his trail of broken whisky bottles!

But once in a while, glasses did clink and drums did roll when melodies flowed during festivities or social get-togethers that happened in the clubhouse. Be it the Navaratas, Ganesh Chaturthi, New Year, or Christmas celebrations, residents gathered to raise a toast to the festive spirit and engage in some fun and frolic. Partying happened side-by-side with trashing, with zero compliance with waste segregation rules. "Why was it so difficult to enforce discipline in any aspect of social living here?" Urmila thought to herself.

When Urmila chose to be a volunteer for the segregation drive, she was faced with the stereotype rebuttal from non-compliant residents: "Urmila, these are high-grade plastics. Why can't they be used to line our bins?" Or to the effect of, "I am following all guidelines. Why should my flat appear in the defaulters' list?" The worst case of callous attitude towards the drive was when sanitary waste was strewn or flung from balconies.

"What on earth is that hanging onto the branch of the tree, Urmi?" her buddy had asked, pointing towards the tree that grew near the shaft area of Tower 1. Both Urmila and her comrade in the waste segregation drive were touring the premises. "It is definitely not a flower. Could it be a dead bird or something? Come, let us take a closer look." At that moment, one of the housekeeping staff sweeping that area came up to them and said, "Madam, so many times, I see napkins thrown like this, especially in that area", she said, pointing towards the litter in the shaft." Urmila and her friend exchanged glances. Her friend replied to the lady in Kannada, "We will take care!"

While the age-old adage "Cleanliness is next to Godliness" seemed to resound amongst residents when highlighting unkempt common areas—be it the elevator, staircase landings, the shaft space, the OWC with flies' infestation, the pestilence in the basement, and the swimming pool—what fell on deaf ears was the universal principle: 'You cannot bury your trash in the neighbourhood, and expect to find treasure in home grounds'.

"It is like you create a mini landfill outside our apartment and expect no foul odours to invade us. Or, have chain smokers on your floor and expect to breathe clean air." Urmila was discussing this fervently with her walking companion. "Community living is an ecosystem on its own, and we are socially interdependent. How each one of us treats our environment comes back to us tenfold.

You get what you give." she continued but stopped midway as her buddy held her hand back to prevent her from taking the next step forward. "Pet poop!" she cried in dismay. They took a picture so that it could be circulated in the exclusive pet parent WhatsApp group of PMS.

The pet poop affair came out in the open in the relevant groups. The poop infestation was discussed at length, including how it had permeated the clubhouse swimming pool as well. The toddlers' pool was under the cynosure of all eyes. The recurrence of floating poop in the toddlers' pool was playing foul with the community's sense of hygiene. The pool was therefore shut down for a couple of days to undertake heavy-duty maintenance. As this had happened during the summer holidays, the debate on poop in the pool picked up heat. With the buck passed from pet parents to toddlers' parents, the aggrieved and vociferous residents, who would rather have luxuriated in the infinity pool, took to playing WhatsApp Polo. From pets to toddlers to unmindful pet parents and callous human parents, the rolling ball bounded and rebounded to no goal in sight. When the moment of refereeing came in to disband the virtual brawlers, the buck stopped being passed. "What is the MC doing instead of enforcing rules? Sleeping happily?" The comment roared loud and clear through the mess of poop, unsegregated garbage issues, poopy pools and exposure to health hazards, and contaminated water seeping through sources of drinking water right up to the overhead tanks!

The heated discussions had left Urmila with a mix of feelings. She was tickled and tired at the same time. Vats had just returned from an inspection of the pool area with Snape. They had wanted to check the pipelines to the overhead tanks and inspect the testing that was going on there.

While nibbling on an already delayed lunch, he was casually giving updates to Urmila. "It is utterly false; the information about water supplies between STP and fresh water getting mixed up. These people are such rumour mongers! Creating a ruckus for nothing!"

"Well, one's flight of imagination flies higher than the 19th storey of the building. I am sure the plumbing lines of PMS have no such overlaps. Or, it is not that the rusted exterior breaks one fine day, and we will experience a waterfall, would it?" Urmila said it with a nervous laugh. Even she knew that she could not hide the shadow of doubt or her scepticism about 21st-century plumbing works.

# EGOs that Bloat up to 19 stories – Like Bubbles and Hot Air Balloons

Against gravity, water columns rose 19 stories high where the overhead tanks were kept on the terrace of PMS. The terrace was a maze of pipelines, navigating around eight massive water tanks. Access to the terrace was restricted; it was locked most of the time for safety reasons. But that did not thwart the thrill-seeking teenagers of PMS, who would go so far as to break into the terrace. They were even caught taking selfies standing near parapets or seated on the overhead tanks, past the twilight hour. Urmila wondered whether these high-rises gave her the feeling of being atop a mountain. The terrace also became a secret hangout for adolescents who wanted to covertly invite their dates and make out, away from the prying eyes of their parents!

One such incident that received immediate attention from the MC was the case of an adolescent who was found in a compromising position with her boyfriend on the terrace. Urmila did not have to jostle her memory to remember every single detail of the episode. Vats was taken into confidence about the incident. Only three people in the MC—Snape, Vats, and the "She" knew about the episode, and they desperately sought Vats' viewpoint on this. The honour and dignity of an exposed adolescent seemed to hang onto the ledge of the terrace of the PMS building.

No sooner had Vats arrived from his office, Snape buzzed him immediately. Snape's antennae about incoming and outgoing residents of 'interest' were the cameras in the lift and the MYGate notifications, which he was tuned into 24*7. Urmila had figured this out when Vats was pinged by clockwork, ten minutes after his arrival from his office. This could not have been sheer coincidence; Urmila declared this to Vats. "Urmi, I think that is stretching it a bit far. I'm sure this guy has office work to do as well."

But the SOS this time sounded five minutes earlier than usual. Snape had allowed Vats, a breathing space of five minutes, to be exact, for settling down. "Must be something important", Vats dislodged himself from the couch. "You have your dinner. Don't wait for me." Vats told Urmila and went down for the meeting.

When he came back, Urmila did not wait for him to slump on the couch. She wore a questioning look. "Now, what, Vats?" Vats briefed her about the incident. Urmila was appalled and, at the same time, pensive, as she too had two adolescent children. "What is coming to be of the younger generation, Vats? No moral bounds, no restraint..." she trailed off as Vats' phone rang. It was Snape on call.

Snape wanted Vats to initiate the conversation with the child's mother, as it was extremely critical that the issue be handled with sensitivity. Though both the "She" and Snape did not explicitly acknowledge Vats' people skills, as evident in resolving issues with previously engaged Facility Management Services, residents, and other third-party vendors, they knew he was the right person to put at the forefront. This invisible conviction of theirs was evident from their repeated requests for Vats to be present in the meeting.

There were discussions, tele-talks, and a final round of meet-ups involving just Snape, the "She" and Vats to decide the course of action. Every stage of Vats' involvement in this issue was cast-ironed in Urmila's memory. With time stamps of the chain of events, starting February 20, 2023. This date would be historic in the lives of both Urmila and Srivatsan. Just five days later, Vats was notified that he had been accused of harassment by the two lady staff from the Maintenance team.

*From Vats the confidant in a sensitive, women-centric issue to Vats the violator of women's rights, this was an unfathomable contradiction. Yet, this contradiction prevailed over the public opinion, the social influencers, and the succeeding MC members, who were not willing to step beyond the shadow created by Snape and his clout.*

What continued to gnash at Urmila like the excess acid in her gut was that the residents, not affected by any of the societal issues, were in a bubble-wrap existence. They did not want to step out of their bubbles. Those who considered it beneath their ego and pride to get involved in such matters, especially cases of harassment, decided to break the tether with society. These residents, in the wake of such social crises, would go clambering onto their imaginary hot air balloons and fan their 'flaming' egos under the presumption that they would never need to descend to mingle with the earthlings of PMS. Some of these hot air balloon riders would not mind waving their flags of support for the majority. And those who participated on the ground were the crowd in Snape's cloud of megalomania. Urmila felt castaway on a 'nowhere' island, with mists creeping upon her and the chillness of the surrounding trees on that island rustling in an ominous tone, "DOOM on you!"

# Exile!

"Leave it, Srivatsan. Don't drag this further. In a few months, people will also forget that this incident happened. The more you rake it up, the more these clowns will keep trashing your name and reputation." suggested one of the residents, who was also part of the anti-Snape squad in PMS.

"Reputation, huh?" Urmila asked Vats with a shadow of sarcasm when she learned about what the anti-Snape squad member had to say. She continued, "Rudy is on a rampage. He is circulating the recordings – the so-called 'evidence' to every resident who is raising doubts about the investigation. Can we even continue living here?"

"Don't talk like that, Urmi. If we do that, it will only show that we are in the wrong. People will get to know the truth one day. Let the court of law decide."

"You know what, Vats. Our photos have been circulated as well. This I got to know from one of my acquaintances, who bumped into me yesterday. Whenever I go down, which is very rare these days, I am stared at, as if I am some rare wildlife species that has come out in the open. I feel estranged in our own home, Vats. Those with whom I would exchange casual pleasantries turn away, as if they were avoiding a blight. Forget our premises. In the movie theatre last week, I realised that the family sitting next to us was the current MC's president and his wife. You can easily guess what would have followed. Heads nogging, hubby and wifey engaging in Chinese whispers, "It is them," and the wife popping her head out to have a clear look. Unfortunately, I could not even move to any other seat as it was housefull."

"And those housekeeping ladies, they stomp around the premises like British royalty. I am pretty sure that they have gotten a whiff of the proceedings of the GBM, as they have the airs of one who has trampled over someone's remains. Every time I go into the FM room to report plumbing or power issues, they give the most audacious reply. It is evident Snape & Co. are mollycoddling them."

"It is no surprise because, wherever Snape is involved, there is no code of morality or integrity. He will go to any level to satiate his ego. He is highly crooked", declared Vats as he tried to sort through the sheaf of papers lying on his desk. While doing that, he carefully kept the Treasury document folder aside. Urmila could sense an enforced detachment from Vats towards the same. Vats had put his heart and mind into streamlining many processes in the association. He was engaged with the staff and his role and never minded stepping up, even for late-night duties. Neither of them expected a medal for the honorary job being undertaken but trashing someone's honour like this! Urmila felt her being pulled apart, like going through 'Hang, draw, quartering," the infamous practice of mediaeval times to punish the guilty. Being treated like a social pariah was not one bit acceptable. She could not stomach the anger, the appalling unfairness, and the compulsive silence on the issue from her end, as Vats had taken legal recourse. Seething with feelings of helplessness, her repressed anger slowly started to consume her.

******

# Bottled-up – The Storm in a Teacup

The bottle, with its tightly screwed lid, lay there on the dining table, its contents glistening under the morning sun. They looked like gemstones, extricated from the depths of the earth and carefully polished to become the status symbol of a woman, who would flaunt it unabashedly in her social circles. But for a woman who had been blindfolded and led to an abyss of social outrage, isolation, and animosity, the sparkle from these gemstones only made it even more insufferable. Just like a death row inmate who is about to be executed is allowed to see the light of day for one last time but shies away from the blinding glare, Urmila groggily pushed away that bottle from her sight and downed the blinds of the window in the dining room.

"They roam around guiltlessly. And those housekeeping ladies, they loiter scot-free! How can they not bear any responsibility for the damage they have done? O' Doctor, how can creatures like Snape even exist?"

Urmila had lamented to her therapist during her first visit. Urmila's anxiety, anger, and repression had finally manifested into severe gut distress. Irritable bowels, bouts of vomiting, and brain fog. These were red flags to prompt Urmila to see the doctor.

It had been almost four months since the eruption of the episode. Vats' advocate had issued the court notice to the "Tedious Trio"—the "She", Rudy, and Snape. The order had contested Vats' dismissal from the committee. It had riled the trio up a good deal. An SGM was conducted to seek the owners' support to fight the case against Srivatsan. The elderly league present at the SGM tried to remonstrate calmly with the other aggressors. But they were hushed. Srivatsan had gone to the meeting to explain the court order. Later, as the crowd was starting to disperse, Srivatsan had a separate conversation with the elderly. He explained, "Sir, my name has been tarnished in the auditors' and GST offices. I was left with no choice. I had repeatedly asked these people to withdraw the notice, but they would not budge."

Urmila, at the time of the meeting, as had been her ritual for the past four months, was circumambulating the shrine of Lord Hanuman at the temple to help her family through the dire crisis. Her condition was similar to, to quote the famous poet, Shelley, "As thus with thee in prayer in my sore need."

Every day of anticipation about what diabolical designs Snape and his clout will be hatching with their lawyer had not only worn out Urmila but turned her into a nervous wreck. She had begun to suspect the maintenance company staff, who would visit for recurrent plumbing or electrical issues. Would they deliberately sabotage the water or power supply? They had the controls, after all. Or worse, would they try to record the conversations with them, just at Snape's bidding? When confessing her fears to Vats, he would just chide her, "Urmi, you are letting this get to you. They won't have the guts to do anything of that sort. We will cross the bridge when we come to it. Let us just wait for the time being." Urmila had stopped going for evening walks, which she would never miss for anything. Her daughter had faced a lot of scathing remarks on the school bus as she and Rudy's daughter were in the same school. As for her son, he stopped going down to play altogether.

As she once confided to her therapist, "It is like I have been stripped and paraded threadbare whenever I step out of my house, passing the common pathways or the ground. The way I am gawked at by those people, especially Rudy, whenever he walks his dog, I get that gnawing feeling in my gut that makes me want to cry, but tears refuse to flow."

"What's more, the b*tch housekeeping lady called me a mad woman. When I confronted her about framing my husband, she called out, 'Learn to control your husband before you raise questions to me!'"

"It is insulting to the core, Doctor. It is just unbearable, and I sometimes feel like I need to end it once and for all."

The therapist seemed to assimilate what Urmila was trying to say. And while replying, she chose her words carefully, weighing them in. "Urmila, yes, it can be extremely painful to feel banished, as you say by your society. But this is just a phase. The control is within you and how you react to it, Urmila. You are a mother and a pillar of strength for your family. You have shared your past and the adversities that you have faced in life. You have been resilient through all of it. That should be your source of strength now. As for society and the crowd, today, you feel they are against you. Tomorrow, they might be against those perpetrators. You just cannot validate your self-worth based on what society thinks of you. No, we are more than what others think of us. Our honour does not lie in others' perceptions of us. You should try to outgrow it, Urmila."

"I am not sure, Doctor. It is just the rage of putting me and my family through so much trauma. Were we wrong in taking a stand against them? Or do we live in dysfunctional societies that are so impervious to what happens to a fellow resident? Can the hankering for authority and fame be so depraved that you do anything to come to power?"

Suddenly, Urmila stood up, clenching the headrest of the chair, her knuckles turning white. She felt a surge within her. "OR ARE WE SO DUMB TO JUST BLINDLY BELIEVE... OR IS IT A MATTER OF SOCIAL ACCEPTANCE TO JUST DO WHAT THE MAJORITY SAYS? NOT EVEN A SINGLE PERSON COULD THINK OR VOICE THAT MY HUSBAND WAS FRAMED. THOSE LADIES AND THAT F*CKING A**H*LE HAD COLLUDED. They all conspired, doctor. NOT ONE PERSON FROM THE SOCIETY VOICED THAT WE WERE WRONGED... THEY CALLED MY HUSBAND A PREDATOR." Urmila collapsed at that instant. She looked like the wrung linen on a clothesline, which, after holding too long in the stormy weather, gave in to the current.

Before she completely lost consciousness, Urmila uttered, "Even if somebody is gang-raped or murdered in our society, the residents will remain indifferent! ...." Blood had spewed from her mouth as she fell limply to the floor and blacked out.

# Redemption, Resurrection, and a Case in Progress

The gemstone-like things on the bare tabletop yet again caught Urmila's attention. Urmila felt like toying around with it. She spun it around, like a spin top, just to see if the contents of the bottle would diffuse into the dizziness of a topsy-turvy world. Just a month ago, Urmila had 'diffused' into the chaotic swirl that had clouded her life - by completely shutting down at her therapist's clinic.

But Urmila noticed that no sooner did the spin stop, the contents of the bottle settled down to normalcy. The inertia of the bottle's contents had come into play to battle the outside forces and come to its original state of equilibrium. "Why can't I, then?" Urmila asked herself, taking the bottle in her hands. She could still not make out whether the anti-anxiety pills she was holding in her hands were actually one 'gem' of curatives or were they just rendering the placebo effect. She had started to feel better, just as her therapist had assured her. But more than those pills, what helped clear the mists of her mind was a spark that had ignited during her moment of revival. The collapsing incident at the clinic saw her being rushed into a medical emergency.

With doctors hovering around prescribing medicines for acute reflux and anti-anxiety pills, Urmila realised that she was not yet ready to become a patient in a closed, chloroform-conditioned, white-plastered hospital room. She mustered up the spirit to think ahead. She might never be able to fulfil a dying wish of jumping on Snape, Rudy, and the "She" with hobnailed boots, but then there was a way of dunking them in a boiling vat of regret and shame.

She would write. She would characterise them into the most compelling story depicting the dark side of gated communities and modern societies. Urmila knew that writing can be cathartic. With the power of words, she would express her angst about the gross unfairness of a system, and probably awaken the living dead to the grotesque reality, which, if left unseen and unheard, would engulf them too, just like quicksand.

The plot of her story would be centred around the allegations against Vats. The conspirators, with their mafia-like tendencies, could be exacerbated as sociopaths. The two ladies, especially Slime with her dubious credentials of Indian citizenship ("Could she have been a part of a terror network?", Urmila wondered, with what had come to the fore, with regard to Slime's dalliance, and her dubious credentials of Indian citizenship) and Parashakti had to be investigated with thorough background check, primarily tracing communication links between them and Snape. Whether the current MC was siphoning off funds to the two ladies to present a case against Vats. As for Vats, would he be the anti-hero of the story? What end will fit the story, with the case in court still pending? I can draw out the most unexpected twist..." Here, while wringing her thought processes for a conceivable plot, Urmila stopped abruptly. She heard loud footsteps from the corridor leading to the front door of her apartment.

"Mom, we are back home," was the announcement that followed the clicking of the front doorknob. Urmila looked fondly at her laptop screen and the writing pad, which was lying on the side table. Her pen's ink started to flow freely after a few shakedowns. Urmila was set for her journey ahead. To tell a riveting story of modern society—its myriad shades and the dark side—that will stir the hearts of her readers.

She got up to greet her children, but before she proceeded to the living room, where she knew her kids would have slouched, she took one last look at the bottle of 'gems'. They looked fiery now, ready to burst into energy from their bottled-up state. They finally had the placebo effect on Urmila, and she had resurged from the recesses of gloom and doom. Urmila was ready to fight back, after these six long months of mental trauma.

The post-afternoon sun bathed her bedroom in golden light. The warmth seeped through the ethos of her room along with a glimmer of hope, and Urmila viewed the familiar walkways of PMS not with the usual feeling of revulsion but with cool detachment to tread a new path altogether!

## *Heights 'n highs - Can we connect, sans the Bluetooth?*

*Homes walled out from climate crisis, pollutions, landfills or forest-fires*

*Defying gravity, these high-rises can be unfazed by any adversity!*

*The blue pools shimmer alongside glass walls and manicured lawns -*

*the fountainheads of novelty spring up*

*The houses of bare necessities fluff up in a façade of flamboyance*

*Flaunting power and money, in unabashed extravagance!*

*Even as trees fall, dust clouds, or rivers run dry,*

*The dearth of water, power or light, can never reach those heights!*

*Powered-up, the high-rise houses wired in a grid of sorts –*

*Connected yet cut off from reality*

*Where both homes and homo sapiens float like satellite isles,*

*In an artificial simulation of nature,*

*The motor drones on and on, till the wires snap off -*

*The pause is like those moments hanging still in an elevator*

*Dark and silent but for a beep - like a heart in a ventilator -*

*Devoid of oxygen in the heights, can you hear*

*the humanness flatlining in an electric impulse!*

www.ingramcontent.com/pod-product-compliance
Lightning Source LLC
LaVergne TN
LVHW041134150826
845673LV00007B/2320